Steck-Vaughn
POINT
of
VIEW
Stories

Rumpelstiltskin

A Classic Tale

Retold by
Dr. Alvin Granowsky

Illustrated by
Linda Graves

D1451386

STECK-VAUGHN
COMPANY
A Subsidiary of National Education Corporation

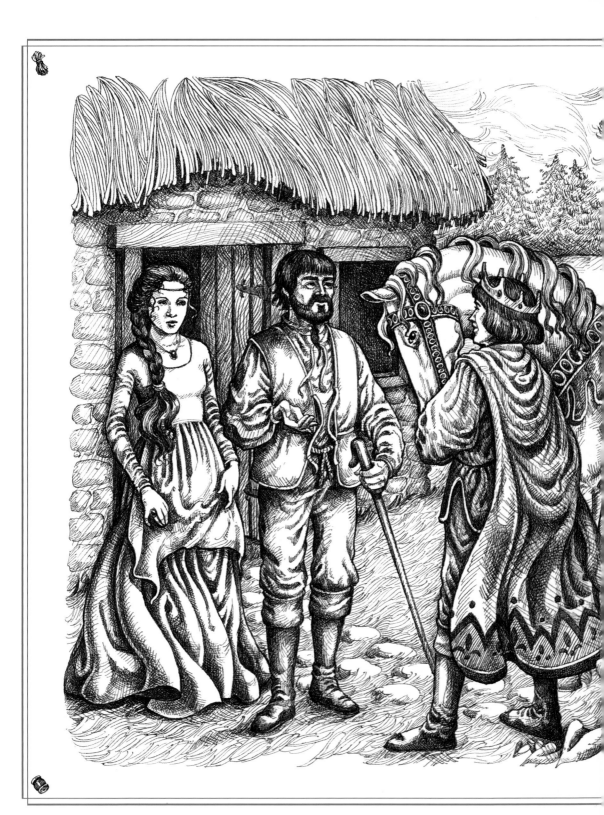

Once upon a time there was a poor miller who had a very beautiful daughter. She was his one and only treasure. The miller took great pride in his daughter and her accomplishments.

One day the king came riding by and stopped to water his horse at the miller's well.

"Good day, sire," said the miller. "What a beautiful day!"

The miller wanted to make himself seem important, so he began to brag to the king.

"I dare say that even a day as fine as this is not as beautiful as my daughter." The miller beamed proudly as he pulled his daughter closer to the king.

"Indeed she is lovely. My kingdom is filled with fair maidens," said the king.

"Yes, but this fair maiden, my daughter, can spin straw into gold!" the miller said.

The king stared at the miller in disbelief. "My good man, what did you say? Your daughter can spin straw into gold? That would suit me very well. If your daughter is as talented as you say, bring her to my castle tomorrow. I will see for myself what she is able to do."

When the miller's daughter arrived at the royal palace the next day, she was frightened. "What was father thinking when he told the king I could spin straw into gold?" she thought to herself. "He knows perfectly well that I can do no such thing. What am I to tell the king?"

Two guards brought the frightened girl before the king. The king led her to a little room at the far end of the castle. Inside the room was a large spinning wheel surrounded by piles of straw.

"You must spin this straw into gold," the king said. "Now begin to work. If by early morning you have not spun all this straw into gold, you shall die."

Then the king turned and left.

The miller's daughter heard the click of the lock and knew there was no way to escape. The room had only one window, and it was barred.

"What is to become of me?" the beautiful girl asked aloud. "I know of no way to spin straw into gold."

So the frightened girl sat alone in the room full of straw and wondered how she could save herself. She had not the least idea of how one went about spinning straw into gold. She tried running the coarse stalks of straw through the spinning wheel, but it was to no avail. The straw merely cracked and split apart. Her plight seemed so hopeless that the only thing the poor girl could think of to do was cry.

Then suddenly the door swung open and in came a strange, little man. The miller's daughter stared in astonishment at her odd visitor. He had enormous feet though he was scarcely bigger than a child.

"Good evening, miller's daughter," the little man said. "Why do you cry?"

It took a moment for the miller's daughter to overcome her surprise and speak. "The king says I must spin all this straw into gold by morning, or I shall die!"

The strange, little man eyed the girl carefully. "What will you give me if I spin the straw into gold for you?"

"I will give you my necklace," she answered. "If you can help me, please do so quickly. Morning is not far away!"

The little man took the necklace and tucked it into his pocket. Then he sat down before the spinning wheel and set to work.

Whirr...whirr...whirr!

As the little man turned the wheel, stalks of straw turned into shimmering golden thread. The spinning wheel hummed long into the night as its bobbin filled with finely spun gold.

At the first rays of morning, the king and his men peeked into the room. Their eyes grew round with amazement when they saw that all the straw had been spun into gold. The miller's daughter sat alone in the room, surrounded by the many piles of gold. The little man was nowhere in sight.

The king was very pleased with his new riches. He was a very greedy man and wanted all the gold he could possibly get. So he ordered that the miller's daughter be taken to another room filled with straw, this room much larger than the first. Even more straw was piled about the room.

"Now spin," said the king. "If you do not spin all this straw into gold by morning, you shall die!"

The king and his men locked the door and left the miller's daughter all alone.

The miller's daughter knew she could not spin the straw into gold. She was sure there was no way out of her trouble. The poor girl could think of nothing to do but cry.

Suddenly, the door swung open. The strange, little man appeared, just as he had the day before.

"Miller's daughter, why do you cry?" he asked.

"Oh, little man," the miller's daughter cried. "The king says I must spin all this straw into gold by morning, or I shall die! Will you help me as you did before? If you do not, then I will surely perish."

"What will you give me if I spin all this straw into gold?" the little man asked.

"I have only this ring from my finger," she said.

The little man took the ring and tucked it in his pocket. He sat down before the spinning wheel and set to work.

Whirr…whirr…whirr!

Once again the little man spun straw into gold until the wee hours of the morning. When the job was done, the strange, little man disappeared.

When the king and his men arrived at the crack of dawn, they saw only the miller's daughter and a room piled high with glittering gold. The king was overjoyed with this new wealth. But being a greedy man, he still longed for more gold.

So the king had the miller's daughter taken to a still larger room filled with straw and said, "This straw, too, you must spin into gold by morning. If you do so, you shall be my wife. If you do not, you shall die." He thought to himself, "If she is able to spin all this straw into gold in just one night, she deserves to be my wife."

Then the king and his men left the room and carefully locked the big door behind them. The miller's daughter was beside herself with grief, for she could not spin straw into gold. She was certain she would soon die. She looked at the huge piles of straw that filled the room and she began to cry.

Again the little man appeared and asked, "Miller's daughter, why do you cry?"

"Oh, little man," she cried. "It is worse than before. Even you could not spin this much straw into gold in one night. The king has promised to marry me if I spin these piles of straw into gold, but if I cannot do it I will die."

"What will you give me if I spin the straw into gold for you?" asked the strange, little man.

"I have nothing left to give you," the miller's daughter answered sadly.

"I will help you," the little man said. "But you must promise to give me something."

"Oh, anything! Anything you ask!" cried the miller's daughter.

"You must promise to give me the first child you have after you become queen," the strange, little man replied.

The miller's daughter was taken aback by the little man's demand, but thought, "Who knows if I shall really be queen? And if I am queen, who knows if I shall have a baby?"

She could see no other way out of her trouble so the miller's daughter promised the little man her first-born child.

In return for her promise the strange, little man hopped to his task at the spinning wheel.

Whirr…whirr…whirr!

The bobbin went round and round. The little man worked until the huge piles of straw were all spun into gold.

When the king arrived in the morning, his smile was almost as bright as the gold that filled the room.

"Ah, you are a special girl indeed," he said. "You shall be my wife—the queen of the land."

He ordered the wedding celebration to begin at once, and the miller's beautiful daughter became the queen of the land.

In a year's time, a beautiful baby was born to the queen. The people of the kingdom were overjoyed at the birth of the prince. Great celebrations were held throughout the land, and the king and queen delighted in their good fortune.

The young queen loved her son deeply. In her happiness she completely forgot about her promise to the strange, little man. Not once did she think of the desperate pledge she had made. Then one day the little man suddenly appeared before her.

"I am here to claim what you promised me!" the little man said. "I have come to take your child as my own."

Fear gripped the beautiful queen's heart. "I am now the queen, and I have the power to give you anything you want. Name the riches you desire, and they shall be yours if only you will leave my child."

"But it is the child I want and nothing else," replied the strange, little man.

The terrified queen began to weep. "Please, is there nothing else I can give you? Is there nothing else I can do to keep my child?" she asked.

The little man took pity upon the desperate queen. "I will give you three days to guess my name. If at the end of that time you do not know my name, you must give me the child just as you promised."

Then the little man disappeared just as quickly as he had come in. Tears filled the queen's eyes as she looked at the baby in her arms. Her heart ached at the very thought of being parted from the tiny prince. How she regretted the desperate pledge she had made to the little man that fateful night!

The queen looked at her baby and said softly, "Don't worry, little one. No harm will come to you. I will make sure of it." She knew she must discover the little man's name for she could never give up the child she so adored.

The anxious queen lay awake all night thinking of ways to meet the little man's challenge. She tried to remember every name she had ever heard. But what if his name was one she had never heard?

The queen was an exceptionally wise woman and reasoned, "If the little man believes I cannot guess what he is called he surely must have a most unusual name." So the next morning she sent messengers to every corner of the kingdom to make a list of the strangest names that had ever been heard.

"Question everyone you meet," she told her messengers. "I must know every name in the kingdom. And do not tarry. I have no time to waste."

The messengers traveled far and wide and scoured the countryside for remarkable names. They registered all the names of the queen's subjects. The queen's messengers inquired in every household in the kingdom and set about recording all the names they discovered on their quest. After questioning people in every corner of the kingdom, the messengers returned to the palace. One by one, they presented their lists to the queen.

The queen read the long lists of names and thought that surely one of the lists must contain the secret name she was looking for.

When the strange, little man appeared the next evening the queen was prepared for him.

"Do you know my name?" asked the little man.

"Tell me, is it Addison?" she asked.

"No, that is not my name," the little man answered.

"Could it be Balthazar?" the queen asked.

"No, that is not my name," the little man answered again

"What about Copernicus?" she asked.

"No, that is not my name," he said.

The queen continued to guess every name she thought might be his. Each time, the little man would answer only, "No, that is not my name."

When the queen could guess no more, the strange, little man leaped into the air and kicked his heels together. He laughed and said, "I'll be back tomorrow and we will see if you can guess my name!"

On the evening of the second day, the little man again appeared before the queen. The queen began guessing even more unusual names.

"Is your name Galloway?" she asked.

"No, that is not my name," the little man answered.

"Are you called Titus?" the queen asked.

Again he answered, "No, that is not my name."

"Maybe you are called Sheepshanks," said the queen.

"No," he replied. "That is not my name."

The queen continued offering names until she had no names left to guess.

"So have you no more guesses?" the little man asked.

"I have no more guesses for now," the queen answered sadly.

The little man was overjoyed that the queen had not guessed his name. He leaped into the air, kicked his heels together, and laughed. "Tomorrow night, your baby will be mine!" he cried. Then he turned about and disappeared.

Now the queen was overcome with worry and despair. She had tried every unusual name her messengers had reported, but none of those names belonged to the strange, little man. How could she discover his name before his next visit? The poor queen did not know what to do.

On the third day, the last of her messengers appeared before the desperate queen. "Honored queen," he began, "I have been traveling all morning to reach you in time to report my news. Late last night I made a discovery. I came upon a fire beside a small house in the woods. In front of the fire, a strange, little man danced. He was not much higher than my waist, and his feet were very large. The little man was singing a song. The words caught my attention so I hid behind a tree to listen."

Then the messenger repeated the words that the strange, little man sang.

> Tonight, tonight my plans I make,
> Tomorrow, tomorrow the baby I'll take!
> The queen can never win the game,
> For Rumpelstiltskin is my name!

The queen could not believe her ears. At last she had the answer that would save her child.

"So Rumpelstiltskin is his name!" she cried. "Thank you, my good man! You will be well rewarded for your help!"

The queen went to her throne and waited for the strange, little man. Soon he appeared. He was most impatient to begin the game and claim his prize.

"Your majesty, do you know my name?" he asked.

"Ah, little man, you have returned," the queen replied calmly. "Is your name Jack?" she asked.

"No!" said the strange, little man. "Jack is not my name."

"Are you called William?" asked the queen.

"No!" the little man said again. "William is not my name." Then the little man laughed and said, "You have only one more guess, and then the child will be mine forever!"

"Well, let me see," said the queen. "Perhaps your name is . . . Rumpelstiltskin!"

"What? What was that?" he shrieked. The little man's face turned red with anger.

"Someone told you my name! Who told you my name?" he demanded. The strange, little man became enraged. He stomped the floor with such force that the wooden boards split open, and he fell through them. The shrieking, little man disappeared into the world below and was never seen or heard from again.

A Deal Is a
Deal!

By

Dr. Alvin Granowsky

Illustrated by

Tom Newbury

STECK-VAUGHN
C O M P A N Y
A Subsidiary of National Education Corporation

My name is Rumpelstiltskin. Maybe you've heard my name before. Everyone else has, it seems. They've heard it from that miller's daughter who decided that just because she became a queen she no longer had to honor an agreement we made.

Well, I say, a **DEAL** is a **DEAL!**

Of course, when the queen and her friends in the royal palace tell the story, they never mention that I was tricked. No indeed! They make me out to be a baby snatcher and claim that the queen is a nice person. Ha! Let me tell you what really happened. I have the time.

Awhile back, the miller and his daughter lived in a little house in the country. They owned next to nothing and were nothing in society. The girl, however, was very clever and very, very ambitious. She wanted to be queen. How could a poor miller's daughter become a queen? Let me tell you. With a lot of cunning and deceit, and with **my** help. That's how!

Someone in the kingdom started a rumor about a poor miller's daughter who could spin straw into gold. Who would have started such a rumor? Well, just think for a minute. Who would stand to benefit from such a rumor? Only one person—the miller's daughter!

Yes, that crafty girl started all the talk about the miller's beautiful daughter who could spin straw into gold. She whispered it to a goatherder, who told it to a kitchen maid, who just happened to tell a footman in the king's palace. Then the footman told it to the guard, who told it to the chambermaid, who told it to the cook, who told the king's own serving boy. The king overheard the cook telling the serving boy. Things went just as the miller's daughter planned.

Now the king loved gold, so the news about the miller's daughter was exciting to him. The king wanted to see for himself if the story was true, so he rode out to the miller's house.

"Are you the miller who has a beautiful daughter who spins straw into gold?" the king asked.

The simple-minded miller couldn't keep up with his daughter. He just stood there with his mouth open. "Spin straw into gold? My daughter?"

"Yes," said the king. "She must come to the castle and spin straw into gold for me!"

Now, that was exactly what the miller's daughter wanted. She couldn't wait to get into that castle. Oh, she was a smart one, she was! She had tricked the king into believing her outrageous rumor. But the biggest trick of all was the hoax she pulled on me.

It all started that first night in the castle, when the miller's daughter was locked in a room filled with straw and a spinning wheel. "Spin that straw into gold by morning," ordered the king, "or you will die!"

Now, how could the miller's daughter spin straw into gold? The fact is, she wouldn't even know where to start. Gold spinning is a very difficult and secret task that can be learned only from a skilled expert. I should know. I've invested years of my life in perfecting the art. After years in gold-spinning school, I served a long apprenticeship. The miller's daughter never worked that hard at anything. No, she was not one for dedication and hard work. She relied on trickery and deceit.

I never tell people about my skill at spinning straw into gold. In fact, I'm sworn to secrecy by my oath to the Gold Spinner's Guild. That miller's daughter must have had me followed or something. Somehow she discovered my talent and came up with a plan to take advantage of it. Not only did she know that I could spin straw into gold, but she also knew about my comings and goings. She found out the exact time I passed by the castle window each day on my way home from work. It was no lucky coincidence that she cried out just as I passed by that day. It was trickery plain and simple.

"What is to become of me?" she wailed. "I don't know how to spin straw into gold, and I am too young and too beautiful to die! How terrible to be poor and powerless!"

Since I'm such a nice guy, I wanted to see what I could do to help this poor girl who seemed so unhappy and afraid.

I went to the door and found it locked. I banged on the lock a bit and the door fell open. Actually, that lock was so flimsy it almost fell apart in my hand. It surprised me because the miller's daughter could have left that room anytime she wanted. I see now that she didn't want to leave that room at all. It was all part of her plan.

When I opened the door, I saw her sitting in a room filled with straw. "Oh, beautiful girl, why are you so sad? What can I do to help you?" I asked.

"Oh, no one can help me!" she cried. "No one!"

"Well, why don't you tell me what's the matter," I said. "You never know—I might be able to help you."

"There is no one who can help me," she sobbed. And then she added in an innocent voice, "Unless you know someone who can spin straw into gold."

She told me the king was going to kill her if she didn't spin that straw into gold. She went on and on about how much she loved her father and her simple home in the country, and about how she didn't want to die. I was so touched by her story that I had no choice except to help her.

"Well, little lady, if you need someone to spin straw into gold, you're in luck. I happen to be trained at that very thing."

"**You** know how? Really? Could you spin **this** straw into gold?" asked the miller's daughter.

I stopped to think a minute. I thought about the oath I took: "I hereby vow never to speak of gold spinning nor to give away spun gold." I had already broken one rule by telling her about my special talent. That was bad enough. I couldn't defy the regulations of the Gold Spinner's Guild a second time by giving away gold. I **had** to ask for payment, but I knew that girl had no money.

"What will you give me for spinning this straw into gold?" I asked.

"I don't have any money. All I have are these simple trinkets I wear. I'm sure you wouldn't want my necklace," she said.

"I'll take the necklace," I said, even though her offer was half-hearted. "We have a deal!"

I went to work spinning all that straw into gold. It never even occurred to me that I was falling into that clever girl's trap. I spent the whole night sitting at that spinning wheel, working while she slept. I remember looking over at her and feeling sorry for her. I just knew she was exhausted from all that crying.

The next morning when the miller's daughter woke up, the straw had been turned into gold. She was very happy to see the gold but eager to get rid of me. I know now that she wanted to be sure that she got all the credit for turning the straw into gold. "Take the necklace and be on your way," she said. "Hurry before somebody sees you."

I was a little surprised that she wasn't more grateful. After all, I had just saved her life. Instead of saying thanks, she thrust the necklace at me and practically dragged me to the door.

I hardly had a chance to look at the necklace. But it didn't take an expert to see that it was made of glass beads and pumpkin seeds. It was worthless! I smiled kindly anyway and acted as if it were a fair trade for a room filled with gold.

That day the whole kingdom was buzzing about the miller's beautiful daughter who could spin straw into gold. Everyone was talking about it. I listened to the outrageous stories without saying a word. I was happy enough just to have helped that poor miller's daughter. I love helping others.

The next night on my way home from work, I heard the miller's daughter crying again. "What is to become of me? I don't know how to spin straw into gold, and I am too young and too beautiful to die! How terrible to be poor and powerless!" she wailed.

I knew right then that the greedy king had demanded that she spin more straw into gold, or else she would die.

Once again I went to comfort the poor girl. This room was bigger than the room where I had found her the night before, and there was even more straw to be spun into gold.

"Oh, you're back!" said the miller's daughter. "Am I glad to see you! Look at all this straw that must be spun into gold by morning. You'd better get started right away."

I was a little surprised at her rudeness. But I figured she was just upset again. I looked around at the huge piles of straw. I knew it would take hours to spin that much straw into gold, but I couldn't leave the helpless girl to face the king's anger alone. Again I asked her to give me a token payment for my services, in respect for the rules of the Gold Spinner's Guild. I asked, "What will you give me for spinning all this straw into gold?"

"You already have my necklace. I guess you might as well have my ring, too, " she said with a shrug.

"All right, I'll accept the ring as payment," I said. So again I spent the night spinning straw into gold, and again the miller's daughter slept as I worked. I looked at the sleeping girl and thought she looked pretty peaceful for someone who had just been crying her eyes out. But once again I forgave her actions. "After all," I thought, "she is only a miller's daughter. Maybe she doesn't know any better."

The next morning when the girl woke up, she rubbed her eyes and said, "Great! You're finished. Take my ring and be on your way. Hurry now, before some wretch sees you."

As she pushed me out the door, she handed me a bent and tarnished ring that looked as if it had been trampled by a horse. But I didn't mind that I was trading a room full of gold for a worthless ring. I felt proud to have helped a maiden in distress, and that was enough for me. I did think she could have been more appreciative, though. I had just saved her life again, and she didn't thank me.

That day people in the kingdom could talk of little else but the miller's daughter who had spun straw into gold. "What a talented girl!" everyone said. "And so beautiful, too! I hear she is also very kind and generous!" Rumor had it that the king was taking a great personal interest in the girl. There was even talk about a wedding.

That's when I started to get a little suspicious about the miller's daughter. I began to wonder if she had tricked everyone in the kingdom into believing she was a sweet, gold-spinning girl. Those thoughts were still on my mind the next evening as I headed home from work.

I was passing by the castle when once again, I heard the miller's daughter crying. "What is to become of me? I don't know how to spin straw into gold, and I am too young and too beautiful to die! How terrible to be poor and powerless!"

It wasn't hard to guess what had happened. The king had demanded that she spin *even* more straw into gold or die. I thought about ignoring her cries. After all, I'd spent the last two nights spinning straw into gold, and I was exhausted. But my generous nature got the better of me, and I decided to help the miller's daughter one last time.

I opened the door and saw a room that was even bigger than the last. And this time there was even more straw than before. By now I knew what to expect from the miller's daughter.

"Hi," I said. "It's me again! I take it you would like me to spend the night spinning straw into gold, maybe while you sleep."

"That would be just great," the miller's daughter said. "It's a big job so you'd better get right to work."

"It's a big job all right," I said. "What wonderful thing will you give me for spinning this straw into gold?"

"Well, I don't know. You already have my entire collection of fine jewelry."

"Well, thank goodness for that!" I said to myself. The last thing I needed was another pumpkin seed necklace. But I still couldn't work for free (the Gold Spinner's Guild, you know) so I had to think of some way for her to pay me.

As I was trying to decide what would be fair payment for my services, the miller's daughter began to yawn.

"I'm really tired," she said, "so let's get this settled. Then I can quit worrying and get some rest. I want to look my best in the morning. The king has finally offered to marry me … as soon as that straw is spun into gold."

Suddenly I realized what was going on. The miller's daughter had fooled everyone so she could become queen. And she had used me to deceive them! Without knowing it, I had helped her scheme along. I felt terrible about the king wanting to marry her. If she became queen, the whole kingdom would suffer. Then, I thought of something even worse—what if she had a baby after she married the king? She would be the mother of the future ruler. If someone like the miller's daughter was going to raise the next king, the kingdom was headed for disaster.

What could I do? I had to find a way to keep that devious girl from ruining the future of the kingdom. That's when it came to me. I could protect the heir to the throne.

I looked the miller's daughter in the eye and said, "Because of me you may become queen. I've done you a very big favor. There is only one way you can pay me."

"Whatever you want, I'll give it to you!" she said. "Just get busy and spin this straw into gold!"

"Yes, I will spin that straw into gold," I said, "but this time you must pay me a fair price for my work." That's when I made my offer. "If the king marries you and you have a child, I want that first child to be mine. I know it is a high price, but it is not every day that a poor miller's daughter becomes a queen! Take all the time you need to decide."

I would like to make one thing very clear. I never pressured the miller's daughter to accept my terms. I warned her to think carefully before entering into the agreement. "You must do what you think is best, but if you want me to spin this straw into gold, then you must be willing to give me your first-born child."

"Oh, all right!" the miller's daughter said. "You may have my first child. Now spin that straw into gold!"

So I spent the night spinning straw into gold while the miller's daughter slept. This time I didn't mind that she slept while I worked. I hummed my favorite lullaby as I thought about the little child that would soon be mine. I would raise the child to be a good ruler—the kingdom would thank me.

In the morning the king was astonished and pleased at all the gold that filled the room. He proposed at once to the miller's daughter. The royal wedding took place that very day. Because of my help, the miller's daughter got exactly what she wanted—she was now the queen.

A year later, a son was born to the queen and the entire kingdom rejoiced. I was the happiest of all because I knew that soon I would have a child to share my life.

When the celebration settled down, I discreetly appeared before the queen and said, "Hi, remember me? Remember our little agreement? I am here to claim the child."

The queen acted shocked. "What do you mean? Surely, you don't expect me to give you my child. "

I was stunned. "Of course that is what I expect," I said. "We made a deal. I lived up to my end of the bargain by spinning all that straw into gold. Because of what I did, you are the queen of this kingdom. Now you need to live up to your end of the bargain and give me the child!"

As I said before, the miller's daughter was very clever. She was able to play upon my pity.

"I love this child so much that I couldn't bear for us to be parted! Is there no way, no chance for me to keep my child? I will give you all the riches in the kingdom. Please just let me keep my son!" she begged.

It seemed like the miller's daughter had changed since she became queen. I really thought she was a distressed mother. What I didn't know was that the loyal subjects of the kingdom adored the tiny prince and tolerated the queen only because of her son. She could not afford to lose the one thing that kept her in their good graces.

Still I refused to accept her offer of riches and wealth. I had my heart set on the child. I knew I could be a much better parent than the greedy king and his high-and-mighty bride.

The queen pleaded and begged. She tried to tempt me with everything possible. Finally, she said something that interested me.

"Give me a challenge and I will meet it," she said.

I was tired of arguing, so I came up with a plan that I thought would give her time to adjust to the idea of giving up the baby. "I'll give you three days to guess my name," I said. "If you can guess my name in that time, then you can keep your child. However, if at the end of the three days you still can't guess my name, the baby will be mine forever!"

When I said that, I really meant for the queen to **guess** my name. I did not mean for armies of her subjects to go into every nook and cranny of the countryside to invade my privacy and search out my name. Evidently she didn't care about following agreements or rules of fair play. She was a powerful queen who could do whatever she wanted. I would soon find out just how powerful she was.

The next day I went to the palace. The queen was very surprised to see me. I guess she still didn't know I was serious about our agreement.

"Hello, Queen," I said. "Do you know my name?"

"Oh my, it's you! Well, let me think. Is your name Addison?" she asked.

"No! No! No! That is not my name," I replied.

"Tell me, is it Balthazar?" she asked.

"Not even close," I told her.

"What about Copernicus?" she asked.

"No," I said as I shook my head.

She guessed as many names as she could, but every guess was wrong. Finally, I said, "You have two more days to guess my name. If you don't guess it by then, the child will be mine, just as we agreed." Then I left.

I went to the palace on the second day. I found the queen sitting on her throne, staring out the castle window. The baby was nowhere in sight.

"Hello, Queen. Do you know my name?" I asked.

This time she had been thinking. She must have guessed a million names. "Is it Cobwebs?" she asked.

"Of course not!" I said.

"Could it be Spiderlegs?" she asked.

"Not a chance!" I replied.

"What about Sheepshanks, Crookshanks, or Spindleshanks?"

"No! No! No!" I laughed. She was getting desperate. "You have not guessed my name, and you will never guess my name. Tomorrow the child will come to live with me, just as you and I agreed."

I went home to my little house in the woods. It was a lovely evening. I stayed outside for a while and sang a little song about how happy I was that the child would soon be mine:

> *Tonight, tonight my plans I make,*
> *Tomorrow, tomorrow the baby I'll take!*
> *The queen can never win the game,*
> *For RUMPELSTILTSKIN is my name!*

It's too bad that the words to the song included my name! You don't know how many times I've wished that I'd never sung that silly, little song. But how was I to know the queen had someone spying on me in the privacy of my own home? How could I have guessed that one of the queen's guards was hiding in the woods listening to my happy song?

When I appeared before the queen on the third day, I was really excited. I knew that I was about to take home a beautiful child to care for and call my own.

"Well, do you want to give it another try?" I asked.

"Is your name Jack?" she asked.

"No! No! No!" I laughed. "Jack is not my name!"

"Is your name William?" she asked.

"No! No! No!" I laughed. "William is not my name! You have only one more guess, and then the child is mine!"

"Oh, my. One last guess. Perhaps your name is . . . **Rumpelstiltskin**!" the queen said, with a cruel smile.

My jaw dropped open. "This can't be! There's no way you could have guessed! Who told you my name? Who told that I am called Rumpelstiltskin?" I demanded.

"Now that I am a queen, my people will do anything for me," she said. "I am no longer a poor miller's daughter. I am a rich and powerful queen."

And indeed she was powerful! Powerful and treacherous! With a wave of her hand, a trap door beneath my feet opened. With a shriek of horror, I fell through the floor and into the dungeon.

For years all I've seen are these iron window bars. I'm locked down here in this damp, dark dungeon because my very existence threatens the queen. I'm here because I know her secret—that she is not what she claims to be.

Now I ask you, is it fair that I am locked away in the dungeon? The miller's deceitful daughter is honored as a queen, while I am dishonored simply because I tried to maintain a simple agreement.

She is the one who should be dishonored, I tell you. She is dishonest and cannot be trusted. She did not follow the terms of our agreement—she did not **guess** my name. Instead she had an army of guards spy on me to discover my name. Any way you look at it, the miller's daughter cheated.

I can't tell you how much I have suffered because of the miller's daughter. Not only does everyone in the kingdom know my private name, but because of her lies they associate my name with treachery.

I know I can never be free again, but I wish I could have my good name back. And I long for the baby who is rightfully mine! But it seems those things will never happen. I guess when you are up against the miller's daughter, a deal is **not always** a deal!